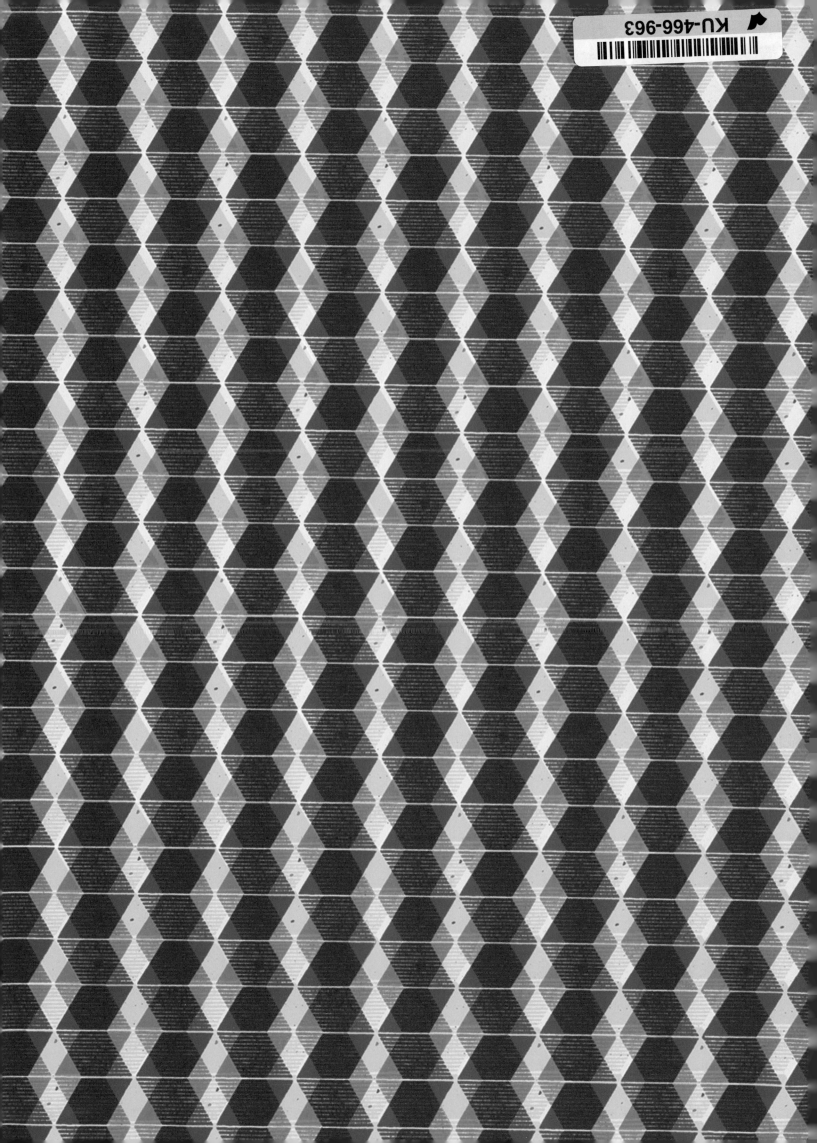

GRACIA IGLESIAS is a Spanish author and poet. Since 1999, she has actively participated in programmes to promote reading through creativity workshops and courses. She has won the Gloria Fuertes, Fundación Miguel Hernández and Luna de Aire poetry awards, and she was a finalist in the Hucha de Oro contest for short fiction.

XIMO ABADÍA is an acclaimed artist living and working in Spain. He has illustrated numerous publications, including *The Speed of Starlight* and *The Language of the Universe* (Big Picture Press), and his work was selected for the Bologna Children's Illustrators' Exhibition in 2017.

A TEMPLAR BOOK

First published in Spain by Editorial Flamboyant S.L. in 2018 under the title *No puedo dormir.*
First published in the UK in 2020 by Templar Books, an imprint of Bonnier Books UK,
The Plaza, 535 King's Road, London, SW10 0SZ
www.templarco.co.uk
www.bonnierbooks.co.uk

Text copyright © Gracia Iglesias, 2017
Illustration copyright © Ximo Abadía, 2017

10 9 8 7 6 5 4 3 2 1

ISBN 978-1-78741-391-7

This book was typeset in Proxima Nova
The illustrations were created with
graphite, wax and ink, and coloured digitally

English language edition edited by Lydia Watson & Phoebe Jascourt
Designed by Noemí Maroto
Additional design by Kieran Hood
Production Controller: Nick Read
Printed in China

I Can't Sleep

GRACIA IGLESIAS
XIMO ABADÍA

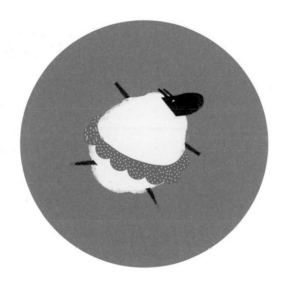

templar
books

Curled up in bed, my head **full** of thoughts,
as night takes over from day.

I toss
and I turn,
I wriggle and roll –
but I just can't drift away.

I CAN'T SLEEP!

Perhaps I should try to count jumping sheep,
or make up a silly rhyme?

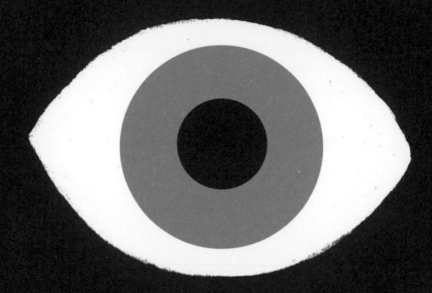

But that didn't work and I'm still wide awake!
I'll try to count slower next time.

I CAN'T

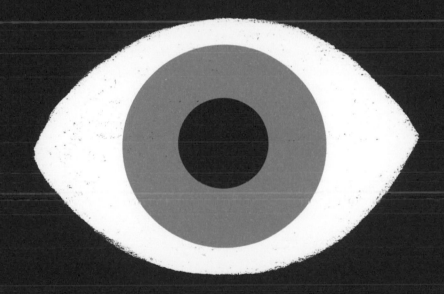

SLEEP!

Ok.

Let's give this a go...

1

A sheep appears from under the bed
and starts grazing on my rug.

2

Another
falls
down
the
chimney,

where it was hiding safe and snug.

3

Look! There's another
– shaped just like a cloud –

floating gently

above my head.

4

The next
sheep is fluffy
— a big cotton ball —
all snuggled up under my bed.

5

An excitable ram s^{ki}ps into my room,
and leaps on my wardrobe to bleat.

6

The next sheep's a dancer,
who twists and twirls
in circles around my feet.

7

The wisest old sheep gets out his guitar, and sings me a sweet-sounding tune.

8

A silver sheep hugs me,

and gently

we sway

in the glow of the radiant moon.

Now the littlest lamb
comes and kisses my nose.
"Goodnight," she says, and then…

my eyes s l o w l y close,
my mind floats away,
just as I reach number…

10

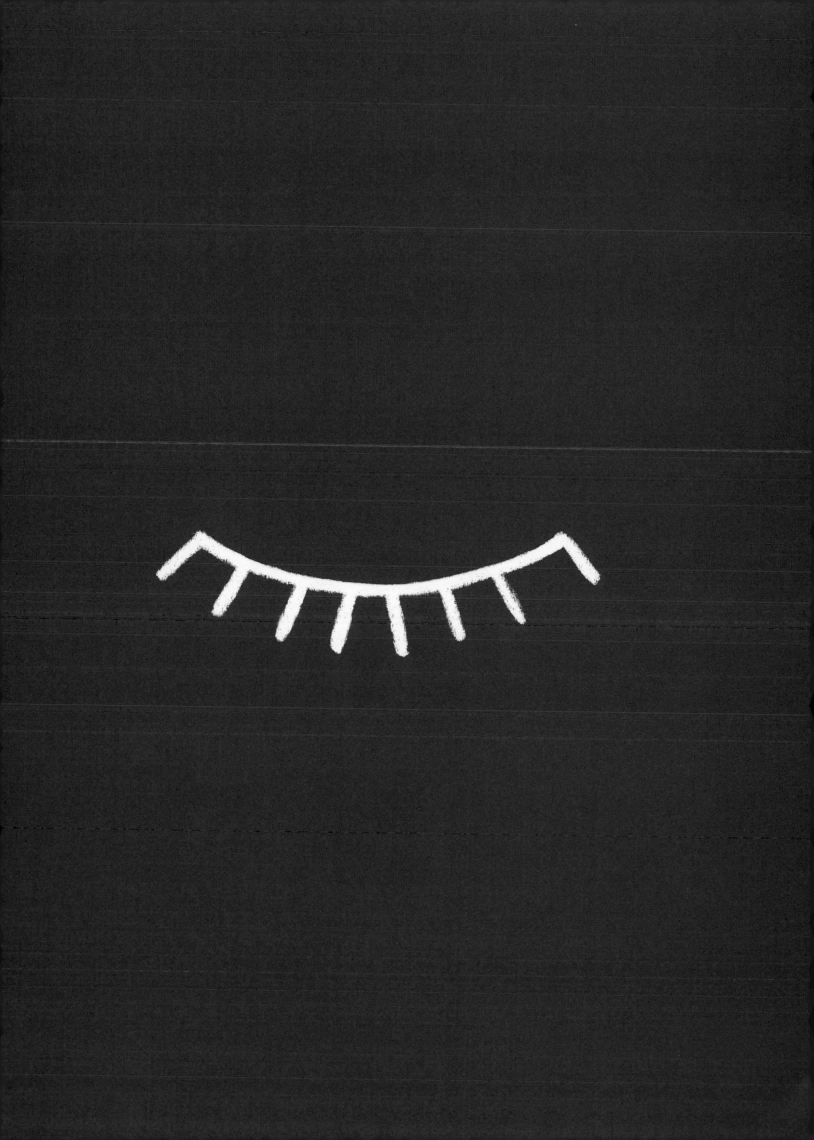

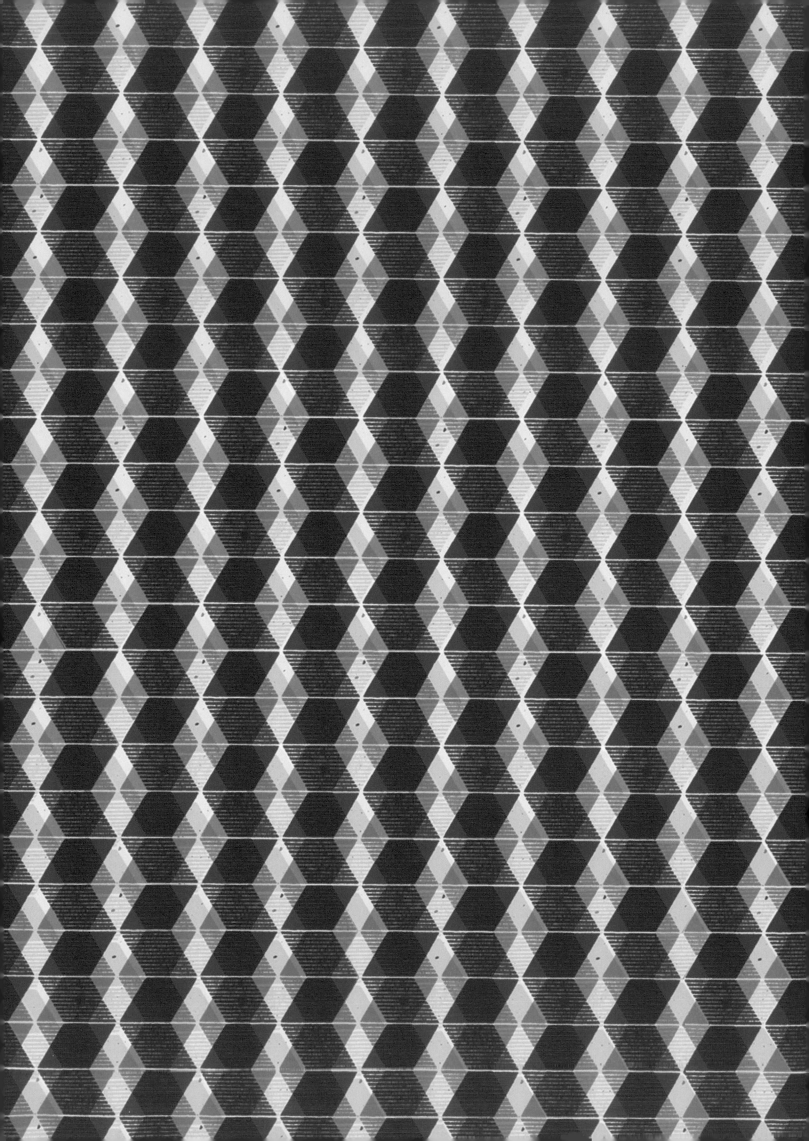

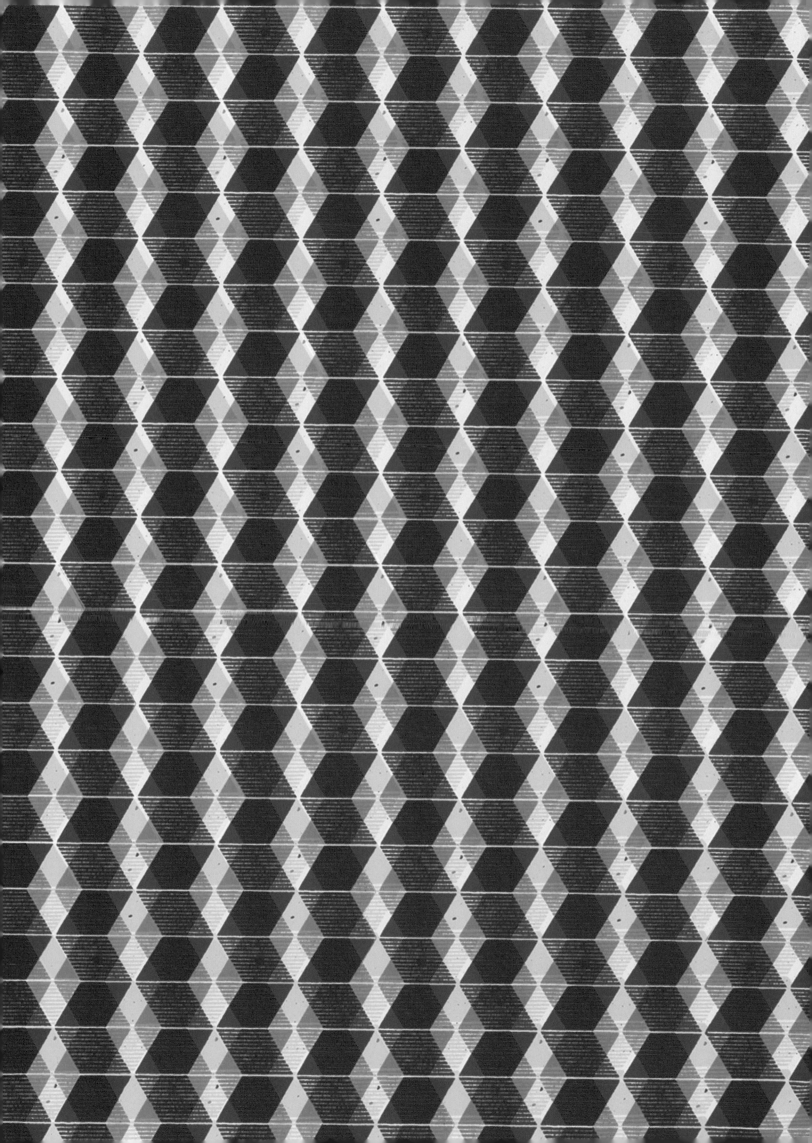

Written and illustrated by Ximo Abadía:

ISBN: 978-1-78741-153-1 (hardback)
ISBN: 978-1-78741-394-8 (paperback)